KB067470

김현 시선

김현
시선

Poems by Kim Hyun

전승희 옮김

Translated by Jeon Seung-hee

POET

아시아

이 책에는 각주 대신 음향과 이미지를 동기화(synchronize)하려는 시도가
이루어졌음을 밝혀둔다. 그런 이유로 이 책에는 국제 음성 기호가 사용되었다.

Instead of footnotes, the poet has attempted to synchronize sound effects
with the images in this book. That is why each poem begins with an
international phonetic character, which is sometimes accompanied by words.

차례
Contents

김현
시선

Poems by Kim Hyun

POET

입추 [ㄲ]

이제부터 원고지 1.4매를 줄여보겠습니다

계절의 감각으로 이야기를 두고

줄거리를 축약할 예정입니다

여름이 사라지게 하지 않고

여름을 이룩하는 것들을 무너지게 합니다

돌과 꽃

돌 속의 바위와 꽃 속의 보

우리는 선명하게 손을 내밀고 있었습니다

그 계절에 무슨 글씨를 그렇게 썼을까요

[ㄲ] 눈은 잘 받았습니다. 다행히 봉투는 젖지 않았더군요. 이곳은 가을입니다. 가을의 마차입니다. 손을 내밀어 불러볼까 했지만 그만두었습니다. 원고에 누가 될 것 같아서였습니다. 전등을 켜면 눈이 보이고 그 눈 속에서 두 사람은 녹아내립니다. 우리의 눈이란 그런 것을 보는 걸까요, 생각하면 계절이 만연해질 겁니다.

ᵑEntering Autumn

From now on, I'll try to reduce my manuscript by 1.4 page.

In harmony with the season's mood
I'm planning to shorten the story.

Not letting the summer disappear,
I'll have what constructs the summer collapse:

Stones and flowers,
Rocks inside the stones and undercurrent eddies inside the flowers.

We were vividly holding out our hands.
What letters did we write so much during that season?

ŋ The snow arrived fine. Luckily, the envelope did not get wet. It is autumn here—autumn's horse carriage. I thought of calling by holding out my hand but decided not to. I was afraid that it might harm the manuscript. When the light is turned on, the snow is visible and two people are melting down in it. Are our eyes made to see that? When you think of this, the season will flourish.

시간과 빛

시간은 단단해지고 빛은 말라갑니다

우리는 봄의 검은 물 밑으로 가라앉고

여름의 꽃잎으로 떠올라 창백해졌습니다

어딘가로 가야 한다면

타인으로 흘러가겠습니다

아쿠타가와 선생님, 그곳은 어떻습니까?

이곳의 아침은 이제 제법 가을인 것 같습니다

파란 매미를 넣어 보냅니다

원 고 재 중

Time and light—
Time firms and light dries.

Sinking under the black water of the spring
And floating up as summer petals, we turned pale.

If I must go somewhere,
I would like to flow, as others.

Mr. Akutagawa, how is it there?
The morning here feels really like autumn now.

I enclose a green cicada.
"Manuscript inside."

^g시인

백 년 동안

새를 관찰하고

단 한 번의 총성으로

그 모든 새들을 쏴아 죽인 후에

그림을 그리고

그것을 잡아먹은 관찰자가 있었다.

^gPoet

After observing birds

For a hundred years

And killing them all

With a single gunshot,

An observer drew a picture

And ate them.

^θ고백의 방향

돌이켜 봐도 차가운 여름이었다

불이 켜져 있었다

불에 물을 붙이고 도망가자!

터널 속에서 우리는 고백할 수 있었고 고백은 되돌아

오지 않았다

터널을 빠져나오자

겨울이었다

식물이 무성해서

눈이라고는 찾아볼 수 없었다

θ 의자를 가져올까요. 의자와 의자를 넓게 벌릴까요. 의자를 두고 벌어진
것에 앉아 의자를 볼까요. 두 사람을 의자에 앉힐까요. 두 사람을 마주 보
게 하고 벌릴까요. 두 사람을 가져올까요. 시간과 시간을 넓게 벌어지게
할까요. 벌어진 것에 두 사람을 두고 의자를 앉힐까요. 의자와 의자는 마
주 보고 앉아 있을까요.

^ΘWhere the Confession Is Directed

Even in retrospect, it was a cold summer.

There was fire.

Let's run away after setting fire to the fire with water!

Inside the tunnel, we could make confessions, and the confessions did not return.

When we came out of the tunnel,

It was winter.

Plants were overgrown,

And no snow was in sight.

Into the river where snowmen drowned,

Children were jumping one after another.

Θ Shall I bring chairs? Shall I space them out widely? Shall I look at the chairs while sitting on the space between the separated chairs? Shall I sit the two people on the chairs? Shall I have them face each other and space them out? Shall I bring them nearer? Shall I space out the time widely? Shall I place the two of them in the space between spaced-out time and sit the chairs down? Shall the chairs stay put, facing each other?

눈사람이 빠져 죽은 강물 속으로
아이들이 휘청휘청 뛰어들고 있었다

물에 불을 지르고 도망가자!

시간의 덩굴을 통과해 갈 때 우리는 뼈에 가까워졌고
눈을 꼭 감았다

가지도 않고 지나오지도 않은 터널이었는데
그곳에 돌로 된 열쇠를 떨어뜨리고 온 것 같았다

우리는 모닥불 주위에 앉아
한 송이 두 송이 딱딱한 불꽃이 되어갔다

꽃을 버리고 불을 쥐고 도망가자!
물 밖으로 나오자 긴 터널이었다

물기가 마를 때쯤엔 고백을 받지 않았다
주지 않고 믿었다

Let's run away after setting the water on fire!

During our passage through the vines of time, we got nearer to bones and closed our eyes tightly.

Although we neither went to nor passed through the tunnel,
It seemed that we dropped a stone-made key in it.

Sitting around the bonfire,
We were becoming stiff flames, one lick after another.

Let's throw out flowers and run away, holding fire in our hands!
Once we got out of the water, there was a long tunnel.

Around the time when the water was all dried, I did not accept a confession.
I did not give, but believed.

°이클립스

소년들 사이에

세 개의 돌이 놓여 있다

흰 돌

검은 돌

흰 돌

소년이 소년의 아름다운 얼굴에 손찌검하고

검은 돌을 움직이고

소년의 얼굴이 흰 돌을 움직인다

찬란하고 아름다운

움직이지 않은 돌은

흰 돌이다

○ 바다 위에 두 대의 피아노가 있어요. 그 조용한 날들 위로 낮이면 어둠이
깔리고 밤이면 빛이 들었어요. 우리 두 사람. 흑백 건반을 누를 때마다 바
다가 움직이고 달이 가까워졌다 멀어졌어요. 인생은 가까이에서 보면 비
극 멀리서 보면 희극. 우리는 멀리 보려고 노력했어요. 멀리서 보면 바다
위에 두 개의 돌이 놓여 있어요. 조용한 날들이 탄생해요. 태양의 교향시,
지구의 에튀드, 달의 녹턴. 우리의 입 다문 목소리.

°Eclipse

Between the boys
There lie three stones.

A white stone
A black stone
And a white stone

One boy slaps the other boy's beautiful face
And moves the black stone.
The other boy's face moves a white stone,
Brilliant and beautiful.

The stone that hasn't been moved is
A white stone.
A colossal moment

O There are two pianos on the sea. Over those quiet days, darkness
descended during the day, and light shined at night. The two of us.
Whenever the black and white keys were pressed, the sea moved
and the moon drew nearer and receded. Life is a tragedy up close,
but a comedy from afar. We try to look at it from afar. You can see
two stones on the sea from afar. Quiet days are born. A symphonic
poem of the sun. An étude of the earth. A nocturne of the moon.
Our voices, from our closed mouths.

거대한 순간이
소년에게 다가와
소년에게 운명을 설명한다

모든 것은 목소리로부터 시작된다

소년이 흰 돌을 움직인다
자연이 얼굴을 돌린다

소년은 흰 돌과 검은 돌을
소년은 흰 돌을 삼키고

검은 것이 다가와
소년의 얼굴을 덮치고
소년의 등이 흙바닥에 닿았다

소년은 순식간에 사라지고
소년은 두각을 나타냈다

굳어진 입술 가운데
진실 혹은 거짓
두 개의 돌이 움직였다

Approaches the boy
And explains Fate to him.

Everything begins with a voice.

The boy is moving a white stone.
Nature turns away its face.

He is swallowing a white stone and a black one.
The other boy swallows a white stone.

When something black approached the boy,
And overpowered his face,
The other boy's back touched the ground.

The one boy disappeared instantly,
And the other boy stood out.

Between hardened lips,
Truth or falsity,
Two stones moved.

가을 물질

벤치 위에
돌 하나

돌을 두고 간 사람의 마음을 생각하는 일이
가을이다 한 사람이

개미들을 보다가
마른 낙엽을 옮기는 개미를 본다

개미는 낙엽을 두 번 떨어뜨리고
그럴 때 그림자가 움직인다

바람이 나뭇가지를 흔들었다고 생각한다면
사람

그림자가 움직여 나뭇가지가 흔들렸다고 생각한다면
바람

⁶Autumn Matter

A stone
On a bench—

To think about the heart of the person who left the
stone there
Is the autumn. A person

Watches ants,
And then notices an ant that is transporting a dried
fallen leaf.

The ant drops the leaf twice.
Its shadow moves then.

Who thinks that the wind shook the branches is
A man.

Who thinks the shadow's movement shook the
branches is
The wind.

돌을 끝까지 돌인 채로 두고
보면 돌은 돌이 아닌 덩어리

그 물렁한 우주에서
단호한 얼굴을 마주한다

그런 얼굴로 가을을 보고
사라지는 사람

그런 얼굴을 가을로 보고
나타나는 햇빛

벤치 위에
흰 돌

Watching a stone as a stone persistently turns
It into a mass, not a stone.

In that soft universe,
A person encounters a resolute face.

The person who sees autumn with such a face
And disappears,

Sunshine that sees such a face as autumn
And appears,

On a bench,
A white stone.

^B자연에 가까운 가슴

열린 창문을 열면

구름에게 다가가고 싶다

오빠의 마음이지요

구름을 보고 있다

밖을 바라보고 있는 오빠의 눈은 흔들림이 없다

오래된 안경이 오빠를 지켜낸다

보고 있어?

태교에 좋은 것을 사다 주자

산, 산. 강, 강. 구름, 구름.

한 목소리가 끝나자 한 목소리가 시작된다

앞으로는 형이라고 불러

형의 마음

눈을 보고 있다

눈을 바라보고 있는 형의 구름은 경제

오래된 형이 밥그릇과 국그릇을 지켜낸다

가난하지?

다 큰 놈이 사람들 앞에서 우니까 참느라고, 창피해서……

[B]Heart Near Nature

When I open the window, already open,

I want to go near the clouds.

That's *Oppa*'s heart.

I am watching the clouds.

Oppa's eyes, watching outside, are firm.

Old glasses are protecting him.

Are you watching?

Let's get them something good for fetus education.

Mountain, mountain. River, river. Clouds, clouds.

A voice ends, and then another voice begins.

From now on, call me *Hyong*.

Hyong's heart, watching my eyes,

Is watching snow.

Economy is the clouds for him, who is watching snow/
my eyes.

Hyong has long been procuring rice and soup.

We are poor, aren't we?

For an adult to cry in front of others—trying to hold
back tears, embarrassed...

Earth, earth. Water, water. Heart, heart.

땅, 땅. 물, 물. 마음, 마음.

한 목소리가 시작되자 한 목소리가 끝난다

앞으로는 종점이라고 불러

종점의 마음

끝을 보고 있다

끝을 바라보고 있는 종점의 부부는 살림

오래된 세간이 새 생명을 지켜낸다

이름이 뭐야

땅, 불. 바람, 물. 마음, 마음.

As one voice begins, another ends.

From now on, call me Last Stop.

The heart of the last stop

Is watching the end.

The couple at the last stop, looking at the end, is keeping house.

Old household goods are upholding a new life.

What is the name?

Earth, fire. Wind, water. Heart, heart.

^人여름 과일

아이를 가진 사람을 만나서

긴 팔과 짧은 다리에 관해 이야기했으므로

생명은 구체적이고 신비롭다

복숭아 네 알을 얻어 오며

몇 번

먼 곳

달을 올려다보았다

이룩되는 자연이란 것이 있었다

그 밤에 흰 매미가 자욱했다

무수한 목소리를 들었다

생명의 날짜를 가늠해 보았다

人 메아리, 라고 썼습니다. 미래가 온다, 라고 썼습니다. 미래는 뽀뽀하듯,
이라고 쓰기도 했습니다. 생명을 잉태한 생명을 보면서 그랬습니다. 생명
을 있게 할 수 있는 생명과 생명을 없게 할 수 있는 생명을 하나의 주사위
에 넣어 굴릴 수 없듯이 과일은 생명의 쪽에서 익어가고 미래는 죽어가는
것들로부터 시작됩니다.

^Summer Fruits

Because I met a person with a baby

And talked about long arms and short legs,

Life is concrete and mysterious.

On my way home bringing four peaches, given to me as gifts,

I looked up

Far away

At the moon a few times.

There was the nature that was being achieved.

That night, the atmosphere was dense with white cicadas.

I heard innumerable voices.

I tried to estimate the date of life

On a night when people who had children drink water.

ʌ Echo, I wrote. Future comes, I wrote. Future like kissing, I also wrote. I did all these, while watching life pregnant with life. As we cannot put the life that enables life and the life that can kill life together in the same dice and roll it, fruits ripen on the side of life, and the future begins with those who are dying.

아이를 가진 사람들이 물을 마시는 밤

어머니와 아버지와
나는 구체적으로 신비롭고
내가 오만했다
태어난 사람들에게 사과하고 싶었다

멀리 떨어져서
닿을 수 없는 것들이 주는 가르침이 있어서
달은 어디로 사라지고 달의 껍질뿐이었다

죽을 때가 다 된 것들이
끝도 없이 울었다

피가 붉게 퍼졌다

Mother and Father
And I are concretely mysterious,
And I was arrogant.
I wanted to apologize to people born.

As there are lessons
That those too far to reach, teach,
The moon disappeared to somewhere and only its
husk remained.

Those who were about to die
Cried incessantly.

The blood spread red.

[a]달과 시온

배 하나
깎았다

둘레는 하얗고
볼록하다

손가락으로 그걸 가리키며
너는 말했다

한숨 자자

천천히 너는 숨을 고르고 나는
네가 고른 숨을 한 입씩 베어먹었다

단물이 입안 그득해서
자꾸 눈이 갔다

^αThe Moon and Zion

I peeled
a pear.

Its circumference white
And rounded,

Pointing to it with a finger,
You said—

Let's sleep a wink.

Slowly you breathed in and out, and I
Took a bite of each of your breaths, one after another.

With my mouth full of a sweet taste,
My eyes continued to return to you.

In a dream,
In the middle of night—

꿈에서
한밤중

남자는 과수원에 잠들어 있고
남자는 남자를 비췄다

남자의 배가 불룩해지고
남자는 그 속에서 희고 큰 것으로 잠들었다

너는 열매를 도모하고
나는 사람을 이룩했다

우리의 눈길이 남달라 보였다

A man was asleep in an orchard,

And another man shone a light upon him.

The man's belly swelled, and

The other man, as something white and big, was

asleep in his belly.

You planned for a fruit,

I achieved a human being.

Our glances looked unusual.

^V부드러운 돌

말이 없습니다

누워서 창밖을 보는 일이 전부인 사람의 심정이란

어쩔 수 없는 날씨도 있습니다

속눈썹과 눈동자와 입술과 손가락과 발가락

끝의 마음

움직일 수 있는 것을 모두 움직이고도

움직이지 않는 마음이란 게 있어서

창의 밖은 희고 과묵합니다

당신의 털신과

굶주린 배로부터 가장 멀리 있는 눈송이와

차가운 벽으로부터 가장 가까이 있는 한 잎이

V 언어가 아직 이룩한 것이 없던 시절에 사람들은 물을 통해 자신의 마음을
    상대방에게 전했다고 해요. 마음이 움직이면 잔잔한 물을, 마음이 가만가
    만하면 흔들리는 물을 주는 거죠. 흔들리는 물을 받은 사람은 안심하고,
    잔잔한 물을 받은 사람은 걱정했다고 해요. 단단한 것으로 언어를 삼은
    것은 이런 이유에서예요.

^YSoft Stones

No words.
There is weather in which the heart of a person
who can do nothing but to lie down and look out
the window cannot be helped.

Eyelashes, pupils, lips, fingers, toes—
The heart is at the end of all of them

Even after moving all the things that can be moved
There is a heart that cannot be moved, so
The world outside the window is white and taciturn.

Your fur boots,
Snowflakes farthest away from the starved belly,
A leaf closest to the cold wall
Fix the last posture of the person lying down.

Y At the time when language hadn't made any achievement, it is said
that people conveyed their hearts and thoughts to others through
water. When your heart was moved, you offered quiet water, and
when your heart stayed quiet, you offered moving water. It is said
that the person who received moving water was relieved, while the
person who received quiet water was worried. This was why they
created language with hard things.

사람의 마지막 누운 자세를 고정합니다

돌이 하나 놓이고
다시 돌이 하나 놓이고
그 위로 부드럽게

가장 가벼워서 무거운 것들이 쌓입니다
돌이 사라질 때까지 지그시
무덤이란 돌이켜보면
언제나 집은 멀리 있고 나는 바라보고 있었습니다
청록색 왼손은 그곳을 향해
오른손은 삶을 부드럽게 움켜쥐었습니다

눈을 감으면
어쩌겠습니까
밥값은 남겨두었습니다

A stone is laid,

Another stone is laid,

And over them, softly,

Things that are the lightest—and, therefore, the
heaviest—are piling up,

Until the stones disappear, gently,

When you look back from a grave,

Home was always faraway, and I was always watching.

While the turquoise left hand was heading toward
the place,

The right hand was gently clutching at life.

If I just close my eyes,

What will there be left to do?

I left my meal payment for you.

†여름 유원

가끔 눈이 멀고
가끔 소리를 듣지 못하는
인간의 삶은 얼마나 평화로울까

장엄한 구름 아래에서
넋을 잃고 서 있는
사람을 본다면
그게 믿음일 것이다

멈춰 선다는 이유로
인간은 때때로 지혜롭고
그럴 때 삶은 자연을 따른다

하늘을 향해
얼굴이 부끄럽지 않은 사람은 지금
인간으로부터 가장 멀고

‡Summer Garden, Secluded and Serene

If sometimes we could not see,
If sometimes we could not hear,
How peaceful our lives would be!

If we saw a person
Standing spellbound
Under magnificent clouds,
That would be faith.

Only because they know how to stop,
Human beings are sometimes wise.
When that happens, life follows nature.

A person who is least ashamed of themselves
in front of the heavens is currently
the farthest from human beings
and secluded deep inside nature.

43

자연 속에 깊숙하다

구름에게 배우는 평화란 이토록 전진하는 것

걷다가

단 한 번

구름 때문에 아,

하고 소리 내어 본 사람만이

여름을 가진다

사람은

서서히 낮달까지

움직인다

Peace learned from the clouds is going forward like this.

Only the person who

Has ever exclaimed—ah—

While walking

Because of the clouds,

Owns the summer.

That person

Gently moves

Even the daytime moon.

^φ포기한 얼굴로

사람을 처음부터 다시 시작하고 싶다

사람의 생각은 말로 무너진다

그때 그런 말을 하는 게 아니었다

얼굴을 포기한 사람은 스스로

시간에 갇혀 편지를 쓴다

벽을 마주하는 일로

사람은 빛과 어둠에 관한 사람을 떠올린다

글이 말 위로 쌓일 때

φ 누워 있는 두 사람의 얼굴 위에 누워 있는 크고 검은 두 잎사귀. 잎사귀에
붙은 붉은 눈동자는 나란히 생사를 봅니다. 생은 밤에 빠지고 사는 낮을
분출합니다. 두 사람은 살아 있고 죽어가는 중입니다. 잎사귀가 썩어들어
가는 줄도 모르고 두 사람은 눈물을 줄줄 흘립니다. 썩은 잎들이 사라지
기 무섭게 두 사람은 죽은 사람의 낯빛을 한 잎씩 떼어내어 서로의 얼굴
에 붙여줍니다. 화사하게, 화사하게.

^φWith the Face of a Person Who Has Given Up

I would like to begin being a human being again
from the very beginning.
  A person's thoughts collapse through words.

I shouldn't have said such things then.

A person who gave up on his face
Writes a letter, locked up in time.

By facing the wall,
A person thinks of another person in terms of light
and darkness.

When writing accumulates in words,

φ Two large black leaves lying on the faces of two people who are
lying down. Their red pupils stuck to the leaves look at parallel life
and death together. Life submerges into night and death spurts into
daytime. The two people are alive and dying. Not knowing that
the leaves are rotting, they shed tears over and over. As soon as the
rotten leaves disappear, the two people take one leaf after another
from a dead person's complexion and stick them onto each other's
faces. Gorgeously, gorgeously.

사람은 마지막까지 사람을 추신한다

손바닥을 내려놓는 사람을 보면
마음을 주게 되고

그는 어쩌다 내려다보는 마음이 되었을까

두 사람은 침묵 속에 매장된다
당신과 그대를 다물어야겠다

얼굴을 포기할 때까지
우리는 무엇을 한 것일까

손으로 벽을 밀어내는 사람과
벽을 손으로 받아내는 사람에 관하여 생각할 때

빛과 영혼이 떠오른다

A person holds onto being a human being until the very end.

When you see a person who lowers their palms,
You get to give them your heart.

What made you feel like looking down?

The two of us are buried in silence.
I should stop calling you 'thee.'

Until we finally end up giving up on our faces,
What must we have done?

While thinking about those who push the wall with their hands
And those who receive the wall with their hands,

Light and soul float up.

정신의 모양

날벼락이었다

정신 나간 아이들이
동시에 울음을
터뜨렸다

이강생 선생님도 울었다
한 마리 오징어처럼

하나둘 물에 빠져 죽고 불타 죽는 데도
오직 한 아이만이 울지 않았다

디지털 속에서
우는 아이들 사이에서
울지 않던 아이가 자리에서 일어나
위를 가리켰다

⸢The Shape of a Mind

An accident out of the blue.

Thunderstruck,
Children, all at the same time,
Burst into tears.

Teacher Lee Gang-saeng cried, too,
Like a squid.

Although children were drowning and burning one
after another,
There was one child who did not cry.

Among children
Crying in the digital world
The only child who did not cry stood up
And pointed upward.

If we concentrate our whole mind on one task, what
is there that can't be accomplished? 精神一到何事不成

정신일도하사불성精神一到何事不成

울던 이강생 선생님이

교실 한가운데 떠 있는 것을 보았다

울던 아이들이 울음을 멈추고

선생님! 진도 나가요!

소리치고

한때

녹색 거북이었고

고동 속 아기였고

바닷가에 살았고

슬픔이 많은 아이여서

뱃사람이 되기는 글렀다던

이강생 선생님이 온 정신을 쏟아 칠판에 적었다

일곱 시간 동안 인생을 후회해보자

Teacher Lee Gang-saeng, who was crying,
Saw what was floating in mid-air in the classroom.

Children stopped crying
And shouted,
Mr. Lee! Let's continue to study!

Teacher Lee Gang-saeng,
Who used to be a green turtle,
Who was a baby inside a marsh snail,
Who lived in a seashore village,
Who people thought could never make a seaman,
Because he was a child with so much sadness,
Wrote on the blackboard with all his mind:

Let's regret our lives for seven hours.

잔잔한 마음

지난 봄

2학년 교실에서 일어난 일입니다

다정한 아이들이

한 명씩 교실 앞으로 나아가서는

자신의 마음에는 있으나

교실의 가슴에는 없는 아이들을 바라보다가

......

저는

수연이에게 말하고 싶습니다

수연아, 일 년 동안 고마웠어

2년 전에는 살아 있던 사람이 2년 후의 자신에게 보낸 편지를 그 자신은
영원히 읽지 못하고 다른 사람들이 읽게 되었습니다. 세월은 늙어가고 진
실은 언제나 승리를 눈앞에 두고 있습니다.

⌠Serene Heart

This is what happened last spring
In an eleventh-grade classroom:

Loving children
Walked up to the front of the classroom one after another

And, after watching children
In their hearts, though not in the heart of the classroom,

...

I
Want to tell Suyeon:

I thank you, Suyeon, for the past year.

⌠ The letter, written by a girl two years ago, when she was alive, to
  herself of two years later, could never be read by herself, but only
  by others. Although Sewol-time is aging, victory is always right in
  front of truth.

봄이고요

개구리가 놀라 뛰어오르고요

아버지와 어머니는 옛날에

개구리알을 먹었다는 풍속 얘기

아이들은 가족들 사이에서

얌전히

옛날 짜장을 먹었습니다

It was spring.

And a frog jumped, surprised.

The story of the old custom

Of eating frogspawn, heard from Father and Mother.

Children, among families,

Quietly

Ate the old-fashioned *tchajang*.

⸲자연스럽게

어젯밤 많은 사람이 달로 묶여 있었구나

자고 일어나야 이루어지는

밤의 세계가 있어

늦었지만, 엄마와 아빠들에게

먼저 가서 미안하다고 말하고 싶어

그때

과일을 먹고 갔다면 좋았을 걸

달고 맛있다고 말할 때

모든 게 낡고 제철일 때

⸲ 과일을 먹고서 생각하면 과일을 먹고서 생각하던 11시 11분이 떠올라요.
생각하게 하는 과일과 생각나게 하는 과일을 먹었던 사람이 죽은 동생이
라는 사실을 아무에게도 말하지 않았어요. 한밤중에 자두가 한 봉지 탄생
했다는 이야기를 할 때면 달이 가까워지고는 했어요. 죽은 동생이 씨앗을
손바닥에 올려놓고 있어서였어요.

☞Naturally

Last night, many people were connected through the moon.

There is the world of night
Achieved only after sleep.

Although belatedly, I'd like to tell mom and dad
That I'm sorry that I went before them.

I wish
I had eaten the fruits before I went.

When they were sweet and juicy,
When everything was old and in season.

☞ After eating fruits, I remember 11:11, the moment after I ate the fruits. I did not tell anyone that the fruits make me remember and that the person who ate the fruits that make me remember is my deceased brother. Whenever I talked about how a bag of plums was born in the middle of night, the moon would come nearer to me. It was because my deceased brother had seeds in his palm.

남겨진 씨앗들은 왜 전부 껍질째로 슬플까

눈을 뜨면

동생이 위에서 내려왔다

Why are all the seeds, left behind, sad in their husks?

When I opened my eyes,

My younger brother descended from above.

ᵁ흰둥이

일곱 살 조카가

떠나가는 강아지 때문에

벽을 보고 울었다

저렇게 하얀 게

남의 손에 가는 게 싫어서

검둥이를 혼자 두고

저렇게 작은 게 멀리 가는 게 싫어서

조카는 떠나가는 강아지를 뒤로 하고

엄마도 싫고 아빠도 싫다고 말했다

ᵁ 가을이는 여름이를 낳고 여름이는 검둥이와 흰둥이를 낳았습니다. 할머니는 어머니를 낳고 어머니는 딸을 낳고 딸은 두 아들을 낳았습니다. 두 아들은 커서 쌀을 불리고 마음을 쓰다가 미움 쓰는 법을 찾아보는 아내와 남편을 각각 얻었고, 한날한시에 어머니를 보냈습니다. 아내를 둔 아들은 한 명의 자식을 낳아 때마다 아들 제사를 올렸고, 남편을 둔 아들은 고양이를 거둬 키우며 겨울이면 자주 동치미와 군고구마를 챙겼습니다. 이들 아내와 남편은 가끔 만나 남편과 아내 흉을 보다가도 어머니와 할머님이 들려주던 남편과 아내의 어릴 적 이야기를 소곤거렸습니다. 어느 밤인가 멀리서 걸려온 전화를 받았어요. 눈이 오더라고요. 눈이 오지 뭐예요.

ᵛHindungi

My seven-year-old nephew
Turned toward the wall and cried
Because of the puppy leaving,

Because he did not like to see
Such a white puppy go with another person,

Because he did not like to see
Such a small puppy go far way, leaving Geomdungi
behind, alone.

My nephew, turning away from the puppy leaving,

ᵛ Gaeuri gave birth to Yeoreumi, who gave birth to Geomdungi and
Hindungi. A grandmother gave birth to a mother, who gave birth
to a daughter, who gave birth to two sons. The two sons grew up,
one took a wife and the other a husband, who are soaking rice in
water and carefully looking up the recipe for thin rice gruel, and
lost their mother at the same time. The son who had a wife had a
son and performed memorial services every year as a son; and the
son who had a husband raised a cat and was often in charge of the
dongchimi radish dish and roasted sweet potatoes in winter. Their
spouses occasionally met and endearingly chatted about the faults
of each other's spouses, but also exchanged childhood stories that
they had heard from their mother-in-law and grandmother-in-law.
One night, they got a call from faraway. It was snowing. Yes, it was.

벽이 있어서 다행이었다
조카에게는

검둥이는 강아지라서
사람의 심정을 모르고
사람들은 강아지의 심정을 몰랐다

조카가 벽을 바라보고 앉아서
태어나 처음으로 강아지 때문에 눈물을 흘릴 때
검둥이는 흰둥이가 잠을 자던
깊고도 넓고도 깊고 넓은 곳으로 들어갔다

돌이 있었다
바람이 소쿠리를 뒤집고

검둥이는 뛰다가 멈춰서서
오랫동안 땅을 보고

흰 참새들이
이 논두렁에 저 논두렁으로 날아가고

Said he hated his mom and hated his dad.

Fortunately for my nephew
There was a wall.

Geomdungi did not know how people felt
Because it was a puppy,
And people did not know how a puppy feels.

While my nephew was sitting facing the wall,
And shedding tears because of a puppy for the first
time in his life,
Geomdungi entered the place, so deep and spacious,
Where Hindungi used to sleep, so deep and spacious.

There was a rock.
The wind overturned the basket,

And Geomdungi stopped in the middle of running
And watched the ground for a long time.

White sparrows
Flitted from this ridge to that ridge between rice
paddies

제법 굵은 눈발이 나부끼는
맑은 날이었다

오래되었으나 남은 사람들은
담배를 피우고 밑을 닦는데

흰둥이는 죽은 것도 아닌데
조카는 어느새 잠이 들고
검둥이는 엄마 젖을 물고 있었다

그날 밤 멀리서
한 통의 전화가 걸려왔다

And somewhat heavy snow was falling—
It was a clear day.

People who are old but survived
Smoked and wiped their bottoms.

Although Hindungi did not die,
My nephew meanwhile fell asleep,
Geomduingi was sucking its mother's nipples.

That night, from faraway,
A phone call came.

동심원

이모 사랑해

왜 사랑해

슬퍼서 사랑해

엄마

엄마도 엄마랑 있는 게 좋지

할머니 고양이를

왜

나비라고 불러

우리가 지나 온

아이들이란 뭘까

삶에 가까운 것과 죽음에 가까운 것 중에서 하나를 선택해야 한다면? 아이가 아이에게 물었습니다. 해변에서는 불꽃놀이가 한창이었고 불꽃놀이가 이루는 것들이 모두의 넋을 빼놓고 있었습니다. 질문을 받은 아이가, 그 많은 사람 중에서 딱 한 사람 그 말을 들은 아이가 얼굴이 노랗게 되어서는 아이를 남겨두고 집을 향해 걸어갔습니다. 그 다 큰 아이를 물끄러미 지켜보던 아이가 하늘을 향해 얼굴을 들자 물이 한 방울씩 떨어졌습니다. 아이는 아이를 어디다 두고 와서는.

Concentric Circles

I love you, Aunt.

Why do you love me?

Because you're sad.

Mom,

You like to be with your mom, too, right?

Why,

Grandma, do you call a cat

Nabi?

What, I wonder, are children

That we all once were?

How far, I wonder, does

◌ What if you had to choose between what is close to life and what is close to death? a child asked another child. On the beach, fireworks were at their zenith and what they created was captivating everyone. The child, to whom the question was directed, the only person who heard the question among so many people—his face turned yellow and he walked home alone, leaving the other child behind. When the child who was staring at the other child, all grown up, lifted his eyes toward the sky, water-drops began to fall. Where did the child leave the other child before he came here?

시간이란

어디까지 퍼지고

우리는

무엇으로 깊어진 후에야

사라지게 될까

울려 퍼지는 망각이란

여자는

불꽃놀이를 넓게 보고 있다

Time spread out?

How deep, I wonder,
Do we become
Before we disappear?

The oblivion that resonates and ripples in concen-
tric circles—
The woman
Is looking at the fireworks rippling out and on.

♭기쁨

탄생한 아이가 문을 열고 나아가서
보니 집 앞 계단에
슬픔이 엎드려 있었다

평소와 달리
지느러미를 흔들지 않고
짖지도 않고
얼굴에 검댕이 묻어 있지도 않았다

아이가 슬픔을 쓰다듬으며 물었다

무슨 일이에요
기쁨을 잃었어
언제 목줄이 풀린 거예요

부모만 한 슬픔이
한참 울다가
아이에게 안겨 잠이 들었다

♯Joy

Born, a child opened the door and went outside
And saw on the front steps of his house
Sadness, prostrate and face down.

Unusually,
It was neither shaking its fin
Nor barking
Nor was its face covered with soot.

The child stroked the sadness and asked:

What's the matter?
I lost joy.
When was your collar undone?

Sadness, as big as a parent,
Cried for a long time,
And fell asleep in the arms of the child.

「안개와 상추

마음을 얻으려다
눈을 뜨니
더 아름다운 것이 있었다

병은 그렇게도 시작되고

남자가 안개 속으로 사라지자
남자는 상추를 뜯었다

바구니에 수북이 담긴 것들이
물끄러미
바라보는 얼굴

두 사람은 살아생전 고기를 든든히 먹은 적이 없었다

이제 누워야지 그리고
따라가야지

ᶠFog and Cabbage

When, during an effort to win a heart,

He opened his eyes,

There was an even more beautiful thing in front of
him.

Illness began somehow like that.

When the man disappeared into the fog,

He picked cabbages.

Overflowing in the basket,

The cabbages stared

At his face.

The two men had never eaten enough meat while
he was alive.

It is now time for me to lie down

And follow him.

한 사람이 녹색 죽음이 가득한 얼굴로 걸어가는
뒷모습

안개 속에서 뛰어오는 검은 개

"그이는 너무 자주 천국에 있어"
"그건 어디서 들어본 시에요"
"맞아 이건 백조라는 시지"

슬픔은 병든 꼬리를 흔들며 다시 안개 속으로 가서
따라 갔다

여보
별일 없죠?

The back of

A man walking with his face green with death.

A black dog running toward him in the fog.

"He is too often in heaven."

"I have heard this poem recited somewhere."

"That's right. It is the poem titled, 'A White Swan.'"

Sadness, wagging its listless tail, returned to the fog

And followed.

Darling,

You're fine, right?

^z눈썹

눈 위에 검은 돌

잠들어 있는

눈이 녹으면

물결이 일고

돌은

눈동자로 가라앉겠지

그때 떠오르는

먼 나라의 꿈

z   폭설의 밤이에요. 흰 새 한 마리가 날아가며 검은 씨앗을 후두두 떨구었
어요. 졸음에 겨운 춥고 배고픈 사람이 그 씨앗을 주워 먹고도 더는 걷
지 못하고 눈밭에 누워 흰 새를 보았어요. 속속 눈은 내리고 속속 눈은
자꾸 내리고 마침내 그 흰 새가 눈밭에 내려앉아 검은자위를 속속 쪼아
먹다가 속속 눈은 내리고 이제 밤에는 눈뿐이고 그 눈이 눈을 속속 밀어
올리며 눈을 뜨는 것이었어요.

^zEyebrow

A black stone on the snow
Asleep—

When the snow melts,
Waves will rise,

And the stone
Will sink, as a pupil.

Then, will float up,
The dream of a faraway land.

z On the night of a snowstorm. A white bird flew across and dropped
black seeds. A cold and hungry man, overwhelmed by sleepiness,
could no longer walk, even after picking up and eating the seeds,
and lay on the snow-covered field, and saw the white bird. The
snow continued to fall and it fell again and again, and, finally, the
white bird descended onto the snowy field and pecked at the black
pupils, and the snow continued to fall, and, now, there was only
snow and eyes at night, and the eyes continued to push up the
snow and open.

ⁱ소설

첫눈이 내렸습니다

하라 세츠코 여사님

부음을 받고

산에 눈이 쌓였습니다

큰 불이 났습니다

여사님은 최선을 다하셨지요

두 개의 시선을

생명과 죽음에 나눠 주었습니다

공평한 일이었습니다

---

i   가난한 그녀는 멀리서 오는 것을 보았습니다. 소까. 멀리서 오는 것이
    있다면 그것이 가까운 것입니다. 그녀는 아버지와 고모를 생각했고 죽
    은 어머니는 한결같았습니다. 소까. 한눈에 새가 날아와 앉은 그녀의 마
    음. 산은 낮고 고요하고 물의 분위기는 물을 수 있었습니다. 소까. 저기,
    새가, 살아요. 그녀는 혼자서 먼 길을 떠나야 한다는 이유로 탄식했습니
    다. 소까. 눈은 가벼이 내리고 감깁니다.

[i]First Snow/Fiction

First snow.

At the news of
Madam Hara Setsuko's death

Snow covered the mountains.
A big fire erupted.

You did your best.

You evenly distributed
Your glance to both life and death.

It was fair—
This life.

---

i A poor girl, she saw what was approaching from afar. Is that so,
sir? What approaches from afar is what is near. She thought of her
father and aunt. Her deceased mother was ever the same. Is that so,
sir? A bird flew right into her heart and settled there. The mountain
was low and quiet, and the water's ambience could ask a question.
Is that so, sir? Well, there lives a bird there. She sighed because
she had to take a long journey alone. Is that so, sir? Snow is falling
gently and eyes are heavy with sleep.

이번 세계는

눈은 말합니다
이번이지?

불이 말합니다
이번인 거야

희고 그윽한 창공 속
검은 새 한 마리

눈을 소복이 뒤집어쓰고
불길을 하염없이 바라보고 서 있습니다

홀로 된 아버지와
늙고 어여쁜 고모

그 사람이
그 사람입니다
잘했어

Snow says,

This time, right?

Fire says,

It is this time, yes.

In the sky, white and serenely retired,

A black bird

Covered with snow,

Stared at the blaze, absentmindedly.

Widower Father and

Pretty old aunt

He and

She are not so different.

Good job.

Really, it was good to be taken in.

Children are coming.

They will burn the money and let it fly.

정말, 잘 속아줬어

아이들이 오고 있습니다
종이돈을 태워 날리겠지요

불은 다 꺼졌어
눈은 다 내리고

이제
늦봄을 보겠습니다

인물과 사건과 배경이
하얗습니다

The fire is all put out,

And the snow is done falling.

Now

I will see the late spring.

The character, the event, and the background are all

White.

시인노트
Poet's Note

2015~2016년 사이에 쓴 작품 중에서 스무 편을 골라 묶는다. 스무 편의 시들은 애초에 '목소리의 미래'라는 큰 그림 속에서 태어났다. 각각의 시편에 각주 대신 음향을 삽입하고, 국제음성기호를 사용한 건 그런 이유에서이다. 보이는(읽는) 화면(글)과는 다른 시공간에서 발생한 사운드가 당신의 창조성에 말할 수 없는 영향을 미치기를 바란다. 하나의 단서를 하나의 예술로 만드는 일에 당신이 동참한다면, 당신과 내가 만나는 시공간에 당신의 것도 아니고 나의 것도 아닌 목소리가 흐르게 될 것이다.

부득이하게 이름 붙이지 못했으나, 이 시집의 제목은 '슬픔의 미래'이다.

I selected 20 poems out of all the ones I wrote between 2015 and 2016. They were born as part of a
larger project, titled "The Future of Voice." That is why
I begin each poem with a sound effect, indicated by
an international phonetic character, instead of sim-
ply adding footnotes. I hope that the sound, born in
another time-space than the visible (legible) screen (writing), has an unutterable effect on your own creativity.
If you participate in the work of turning a clue into a
piece of art, a voice that is neither yours nor mine will
flow into the time-space where you and I meet.

I give this small book of poems the title *The Future
of Sadness*.

해설
Commentary

POET

두고 온 것

장은정 (문학평론가)

아래로 무한히 가라앉는 조용한 돌과 이토록 가벼이 밀치고 떠오르는 꽃잎. 이 상반되는 방향으로 물살을 가르며 활동하는, 무겁고도 가벼운 죽음으로부터 글을 시작해야겠다. 시집을 여는 첫 시 「입추」의 한 대목을 이루는 두 개의 강렬한 이미지는 시집 전체를 관통하며 변주되는 운동이기 때문이다. 당신, 돌과 꽃의 미래를 상상해보았는가. 마치 가위 바위 보를 하는 것처럼 선명하게 자신을 손처럼 내밀었던 돌과 꽃의 존재가 시간이 흘러 "봄의 검은 물 밑으로 가라앉고/ 여름의 꽃잎으로 떠올라 창백해졌"다. 봄과 여름 두 계절 동안 살아있긴 했으나 당연하게도 그것은 죽음이 서서히 진행되는

What We Left Behind

Jang Eun-jung (literary Critic)

A stone sinking endlessly and a petal ever-so lightly pushing up to float—I'd like to begin with the concept of death, so heavy and so light at the same time, and cutting through the current of life from opposite sides. These two powerful images, evoked in the first poem, "Entering Autumn," are repeated and varied through-out the book. Can you imagine the future of stones and flowers? The vivid being of stones and flowers, which hold themselves out like hands in the game of rock-paper-scissors, and over time "[s]inking under the black water of the spring/And floating up as summer petals... turned pale." Although they were alive during

시간이었고 이제는 삶보다 죽음 쪽으로 추가 더욱 깊이 기울어졌으니 이 시집의 계절은 가을이다. 그런데 이 시의 제목에 붙어 있는 음향기호를 따라가면 이런 답장이 있다. "눈은 잘 받았습니다. 다행히 봉투는 젖지 않았더군요. 이곳은 가을입니다." 이 문장들은 아직 오지도 않은 겨울의 눈이 담긴 편지를 받은 적이 있음을 전제하고 그 편지에 답하고 있다. 과거를 거슬러 미리 도착한 이 녹지 않는 눈송이의 존재란 도대체 무엇일까?

당신이 김현의 두 번째 시집 『입술을 열면』(창비, 2018)을 이미 읽은 독자라면 기억하고 있을 것이다. 말한다고 쓰지 않고 입술이 열린다고 씀으로써 입 속에서 이리저리 움직일 혀의 움직임, 성대의 진동이 함께 작용하며 곧 만들어낼 목소리를 앞질러 상상할 수 있게 되었던 것을. 그것은 아직 듣지 못했지만 곧 들려올 것으로 기대되는 목소리인데, 상상력이 만들어낸 아직 도착하지 않은 이 목소리 덕분에 독자는 더욱더 오롯이 듣는 자가 된다. 이는 이제 막 입술을 여는 자를 '말할 수 있는 자'로 만드는 일로서 이때 시는 말하는 자를 더 잘 말할 수 있게 하고, 듣는 자를 더 잘 듣게 하는 장르일 것이다. 그런데 두 번째 시집과 비슷한 시기에 출간되

the two seasons of spring and summer, it was also a time of naturally slow dying. Now, in the fall, the season of this book, the pendulum has swung to the side of death rather than life.

At this point, when we turn our attention to the note attached to the phonetic symbol in the beginning of this poem, indicating a sound effect, there is a reply to a letter: "The snow arrived fine. Luckily, the envelope did not get wet. It is fall here." These sentences reply to a letter, in which snow was enclosed from the winter that hasn't arrived yet. What is this snow that has arrived ahead of and against the current of time, and hasn't yet melted?

A reader who is familiar with Kim Hyun's second book of poetry, If You Open Your Lips (Changbi, 2018), will remember that, by using the phrase "open your lips," instead of "speak," the poet is urging us to imagine the voice created inside our mouths by the combination of the active movement of the tongue and the vibration of vocal cords. It is a voice that the reader hasn't heard yet, but whose imminent arrival is anticipated. Thanks to this anticipated voice, the reader

는 이 시집을 이루는 시들이 "굳어진 입술"(「이클립스」)에 대한 시들이라는 것은 놀랍다. 물론 그 입술의 주름마다 입술을 열고 닫았던 순간들이 빼곡하게 새겨져 있겠으나, 이 시집에서의 입술이 '굳은' 것임을 기억하자. 첫 시가 가라앉는 돌멩이이자 떠오르는 꽃잎으로서의 죽음으로부터 비롯된 것은 우연이 아니다.

　이런 의문 속에서 시들을 거듭 되풀이하며 읽을수록 의미심장하게 여겨지는 것은 「고백의 방향」이다. 터널은 양쪽이라고 하는 두 영역을 가지며 들어갔다가 빠져나올 수 있도록 만들어진 구조물이다. 시에서는 터널을 중심으로 계절이 바뀌는데, 그것이 뒤죽박죽 섞여 있어 기묘하다. "돌이켜 봐도 차가운 여름이었다"는 구절과 "터널을 빠져나오자/ 겨울이었다"는 구절을 연결해서 읽으며 여름에서 출발해 겨울에 도착했으니 터널의 계절은 가을이다. 그런데 겨울로 명명된 위치에서 묘사된 것은 "식물이 무성해서/ 눈이라고는 찾아볼 수 없었다"는 진술이므로 여름에 가깝다. 명명된 것과 묘사되는 것 사이의 불일치는 이 시의 중요한 구조인데, "불에 물을 붙이고 도망가자!" 혹은 "물에 불을 지르고 도망가자!", "꽃을 버리고 불을 쥐고 도망가자!" 등의 구절들

more fully becomes a listener as well. In other words, the poet turns the person who is about to open his lips into a person capable of speaking. In this sense, the poem becomes a medium that helps the speaker to speak better and the listener to listen better.

Contrastingly, this new book, to be published not long after Kim's second poetry book, is composed of poems about "hardened lips" ("Eclipse"). We can of course assume that moments of opening and closing the lips were inscribed fully in each wrinkle of the lips, but remember that the lips in this book are "hardened." It is not a coincidence that the first poem begins with death, represented simultaneously by a sinking stone and floating petal.

As we read the poems in this book over and over again, and keeping the above observation in mind, the poem "Where the Confession Is Directed" stands out. A tunnel is a structure with two openings: one for entering and the other for exiting. In the poem, the season changes around the tunnel, yet this change is strangely confusing. If we connect the two statements: "Even in retrospect, it was a cold summer" and

역시 단어들의 자리 바꾸기를 통해 낯선 효과를 획득한다. 대체 터널 안에서 무슨 일이 일어난 것일까? 그리고 고백의 내용은 무엇일까? 이 시는 그것을 결코 말해주지 않지만 그것 때문에 이 모든 것들의 자리가 뒤죽박죽 뒤바뀌어버린 것이 아닐까?

무언가 말할 수 없는 것이 있다. 분명히 존재하므로 말해야 하지만 입술을 열어 도저히 말할 수 없는 것. 부드럽게 열렸다가 닫히며 모양과 소리를 만들어내는 입술과 대조적으로 시집의 도처에서 발견되는 돌의 존재는 어쩌면 내부로 너무 깊이 파고들어 더 이상 형태를 알아볼 수 없게 된 비밀일지도 모른다. 그저 무한히 가라앉는 것 외에는 아무것도 할 수 없는 돌과 같은 비밀. 아마 그래서 "가지도 않고 지나오지도 않은 터널이었는데/ 그곳에 돌로 된 열쇠를 떨어뜨리고 온 것 같"다고 쓰는 것이 아닐까. 시를 읽는 자들은 시에 이미 적혀 있는 내용들에 집중하기 쉽지만, 시는 쓰지 않은 것을 말하기 위해 혹은 말하지 않기 위해 안간힘을 다하는 기록이기도 하다. 그러니 「고백의 방향」이 끝내 쓰지 않은/못한 것, 터널 속에 두고 온, 돌로 된 열쇠를 힘껏 상상해보자. 이를 알아내기 위해 시인에게 대체 그것이

"When we came out of the tunnel,/It was winter," the tunnel's season should be fall, as it begins with summer and arrives in winter. However, what is described for winter is "Plants were overgrown,/And no snow was in sight," signaling a state more like summer. The discrepancy between what is named and what is described forms an important structure of this poem. For example, notice the defamiliarization effect in the following sentences, in which customary words have been replaced with their opposites: "Let's run away after setting fire to the fire with water!"; "Let's run away after setting the water on fire!", and "Let's throw out flowers and run away, holding fire in our hands!" What on earth has happened inside the tunnel? What was confessed? Although the poem does not state it directly, isn't it because of the "confession" occurring inside the tunnel that the positions of all things have gotten so mixed up?

Something cannot be said here. Since it clearly exists, it has to be said, yet it is impossible to utter it by opening the lips. In contrast to lips, which create forms and sounds while gently being opened and

무엇이냐고 질문할 필요는 없다. 왜냐하면 읽고 있는 나와 당신 모두 가본 적 없는 터널에 두고 온 것들이 있을 테니까. 그게 뭔지 각자 이미 알고 있으니까.

　이 시집을 이루는 시편마다 반복해서 등장하는 돌의 자리에 당신이 두고 온 것을 구체적으로 이입하면서 시집을 읽기 시작한다면 아마도 이것은 놀라운 경험이 될 것이다. 어둠이 들어찬 것 같았던 돌멩이의 내부로 누구에게도 말할 수 없었으나 분명히 존재하는 당신의 바위 같은 경험이 **빼곡하게** 들어찰 것이므로. 그것과 더불어 「포기한 얼굴로」를 읽자. 이런 문장으로 시작된다. "사람을 처음부터 다시 시작하고 싶다" 이 문장이 이토록 강렬한 것은 입술이 도저히 열리지 않는 그 경험이란 심지어 사람을 그만두게 하는 일이었을 것임을 암시하기 때문이다. 모든 것이 벌어지고 난 이후, "두 사람은 침묵 속에 매장된다" 그런데 어째서 두 사람일까? 아마도 '말할 수 없는 것'은 결코 혼자서 벌어지는 일이 아니기 때문에. "손으로 벽을 밀어내는 사람"이 있으면 "벽을 손으로 받아내는 사람"이 함께 만들어낸 일이기 때문에. 이렇게 생각하고 보면 어째서 말할 수 없는가를 저절로 알게 된다. 이것은 혼자만의 비밀이

closed, the stones found throughout this book might signify a secret whose shape it has become impossible to recognize, since it is dug too deeply inward—like a stone that can do nothing but sink endlessly. Might that be why the poet says: "Although we neither went to nor passed through the tunnel,/It seemed that we dropped a stone-made key in it"? Although readers of poems tend to pay attention to what is written in them, poems are also records of a desperate effort to speak, or not to speak, what has not been written. Therefore, let's imagine intensely what this poem, "Where the Confession Is Directed," would or could not write in the end: "a stone-made key" dropped in it. In order to find out what it is, though, we don't have to ask the poet. We readers all have things we have left in a tunnel, which we haven't even entered. And we all must know what they are.

If we read this book while transferring what we left in our tunnels into the places of the stones, which appear repeatedly, it would most likely be a remarkable experience. Your rock-like experiences, which clearly exist, even though you could not tell anyone about

아니기 때문이다.

첫 시에 등장하는 돌이 시집의 말미에 배치되어 있던 「눈썹」에 이르러 어떻게 변화하는지 주목하자. 무한히 아래로 가라앉기만 하던 돌이 가라앉는 일을 멈추고 이제는 눈 위에 가만히 놓여있다. 깊은 검은 물을 가로질러 도착했기에 '검은' 돌이 되었을 것이다. 그런데 이 시에서 오로지 1연만이 현재시제로 되어 있다. 2연부터는 "눈이 녹으면"이라고 하는 가정으로 지어진 구절들이다. 즉 아직 눈은 녹지 않았다. 검은 돌은 눈 위에서 가만히 잠들어 있을 뿐이다. 그러나 이 시는 아직 오지 않은 시간을 앞당겨 상상해본다. 만일 눈이 녹기 시작하면 물결이 일 것이고 돌은 눈동자로 가라앉을 것이라고. 말할 수 없는 비밀들로 **빼곡**하게 가득 차 있던 검은 돌이 눈동자가 된다는 것은 잠들어 있던 눈을 뜨는 순간이다. 아마 "그때 떠오르는/ 먼 나라의 꿈"이란, 그 눈동자로만 볼 수 있는 세상일 것이다.

글을 열며 물었다. 편지에 들어있던 겨울의 눈송이란 도대체 무엇이냐고. 이 시집의 마지막 시, 「소설」은 이렇게 시작한다. "첫눈이 내렸습니다" 이 구절을 읽고서야 첫 시에서 미리 도착해 있던 눈송이가 증언하던 미

them, will fill the inside of the stones, which seemed entirely dark.

Now let's look at "With the Face of a Person Who Has Given Up." It begins with the grave sentence: "I would like to begin being a human being again from the very beginning." This statement suggests that the experience about which lips could not be opened, no matter how hard the two individuals tried, was an experience that made them stop being human. After all that has happened, "The two of us are buried in silence." Why two of them? Perhaps because what cannot be said did not happen alone: because the person "who push[es] the wall with their hands" and the person "who receive[s] the wall with their hands" created it together. Then it becomes obvious why this secret cannot be said: because it is not a secret of oneself alone.

Let's pay attention to how the stone that appears in the first poem changes in "Eyebrow," the penultimate poem. The stone that was endlessly sinking has now stopped doing so and instead lies gently on the snow. It must have become "a black stone," as it has crossed black water. Interestingly, only the first stanza is about

래에 마침내 도착했음을 알게 된다. 즉 이 시집을 읽는 일이 통째로 하나의 터널을 통과하는 일이었던 것이다. '하라 세츠코'라는 실존했던 배우의 부음을 구체적으로 들여옴으로써 이 시가 죽음에 대해 말할 때, 독자 역시 그녀의 삶에 대한 여러 기록들과 더불어 구체적인 죽음을 상상하게 된다. 추상화된 죽음 '일반'이 아니라 이름을 가진 자의 죽음이 기입되어 있는 것이다. 그녀의 부음을 받고 산에 눈이 쌓인다. 큰 불이 난다. 눈이 곧 불이고, 불이 곧 눈일 것이다. 눈은 불에게 묻는다. "이번이지?" 불은 눈에게 말한다. "이번인 거야" 첫 시에서는 미리 도착했던 눈송이이지만 이제 첫눈 내리는 날에 도착함으로써 '현재'가 되어있다. 그렇다면 그 다음엔 뭘까? 봄일까? 그런데 이 시는 불이 다 꺼지고 눈이 다 내린 이후에 늦봄을 위치시킨다. 왜 봄이 아니라 늦봄일까?

우리는 봄의 검은 물 밑으로 가라앉고
여름의 꽃잎으로 떠올라 창백해졌습니다

어딘가로 가야 한다면
타인으로 흘러가겠습니다

the present; the remaining three stanzas are about the time when the snow will melt. In other words, the snow is still frozen. The black stone is quietly asleep on top of this snow. But this poem is imagining the time that has not come yet. When the snow begins to melt, waves will rise and the stone, as the pupil of an eye, will sink. The moment the black stone, which is filled with unspeakable secrets, turns into a pupil is the moment when the eyes that are now sleeping will be opened. "The dream of a faraway land" that "will float up," then, is likely the world that can be seen only by those pupils.

In the beginning of this essay, I asked: What was the snow of the winter inside the envelope? The last poem of this book, "First Snow/Fiction," begins with the simple statement "First snow." It signals that we have finally arrived at the future that the snow that had arrived ahead in the first poem testified to. In other words, reading this book is itself an act of passing through a tunnel. By the introduction of the news of the death of Hara Setsuko, a real actor who has just died, the reader imagines a concrete death together

아쿠타가와 선생님, 그곳은 어떻습니까?
이곳의 아침은 이제 제법 가을인 것 같습니다

파란 매미를 넣어 보냅니다
원 고 재 중

—「입추」중

  이 질문에 답하기 위해 다시 첫 시 「입추」로 돌아가자. 이 시의 음향기호에서는 겨울에서 미리 도착한 눈송이에 대해 이야기하기도 하지만, 이제 막 가을에 들어선 시간에 파란 매미를 보내는 것으로 종결되는 시이기도 하다. 아쿠타가와 선생님에게 부쳐진 편지이니, 1900년 초의 일본으로 부쳐졌을 것이다. 즉 파란 매미를 보내는 시점은 아쿠타가와 류노스케가 살았던 관점에서 보자면 참으로 먼 미래다. 파란 매미는 무사히 도착했을까? 약간의 따스함에도 쉽게 녹아버려 편지봉투를 적시기 좋은 눈송이 하나가 놀랍게도 녹지 않고 그대로 도착했던 것처럼, 파란 매미 역시 여름을 그대로 간직한 채로 생생하게 도착하지 않았을까? 이 시집의 마지막 시가 마침내 보려는 계절이 봄이 아니라 '늦봄'인 것은 지금보다 더 먼 미래에서 보낸 무언가가 아직

with references to her actual life. It is not an abstract, general death, but the concrete one of a person with a name. At the news of her death, snow covers the mountains and a large fire erupts. The snow is the fire, and the fire is the snow. The snow asks the fire: "This time, right?" The fire responds to the snow, "It is this time, yes." While the snow has arrived ahead in the first poem, it finally becomes the present by arriving on the day of the first snow. Then what comes next? Spring? In this poem, after "the fire is all put out/And the snow is done falling," what comes is "the late spring." Why late spring, though, and not spring?

In order to answer this question, let's return to the first poem, "Entering Autumn." The sound-effect symbol that begins it mentions the snow that arrived ahead of time from winter in the footnote; but the poem also ends with the sending out of a green cicada in the beginning of autumn.

Sinking under the black water of the spring
And floating up as summer petals, we turned pale.

도착하지 않았기 때문일지도 모르겠다. 그것이 도착해야만 봄을 경험할 수 있을 것이다. 그런데 그것이 무엇이냐고? 물론 그건 당신이 터널에 두고 온 것이다. 그것이 무엇인지 당신은 알고 있다. 비밀을 만들었던 두 사람이 오래 침묵해왔던 그것을 함께 말하기로 다짐하는 순간, 마침내 되찾을 것이다.

If I must go somewhere,
I would like to flow as others.

Mr. Akutagawa, how is it there?
The morning here feels quite like fall now.

I enclose a green cicada.
"Manuscript inside."

Notice that the cicada is sent to Mr. Akutagawa, who lived in Japan in the early 1900s. In other words, from Akutagawa Runosuke's perspective, the time from which the green cicada is sent is the future, a time far from him. Did the cicada arrive safely? As the snow, which can melt and wet the envelope with even a little warmth, arrived surprisingly without melting, might the cicada have arrived alive and fresh, retaining the summer? Thus, the season of the last poem is not spring, but late spring, perhaps because what was sent from a distant future has not arrived here and now yet. We can experience spring only when it arrives for us. Then what is this thing that hasn't arrived for us yet? Naturally, it is what we left behind in the tunnel. You know what it is, and you will finally regain it the moment the two of you, who created it together, decide to speak about this secret, which has been kept in silence for a long time.

김현에
대해

What They Say
About Kim Hyun

POET

김현의 세계를 이해하기 위해서는 여러 개의 핸드가이드북이 필요할지 모른다. 그의 시 한편을 제대로 이해하는 데만도 꽤 많은 시간과 노력이 소요된다. 그런데 그의 시에는 해석에의 열정을 불태우는 무언가가 있다. 아무리 설명해도 부족한 잉여가 있다는 것이 역설적인 매력 때문이다.(……)김현은 우리의 삶이 단일하게 해석될 수 없으며 아무리 해석하려고 해도 손아귀를 빠져 나가는 해석 불가능의 대상이라는 것을 일러준다.

안지영

문학과 정치의 몸은 각각이지만 마음은 하나라는 뜻이거니와 그것은 양자가 별개로 분리된 존재임을 부정하지 않으면서도 '이질성들 사이의 자유롭고 평화로운 공존'이라는 공동의 비전을 따라 양자의 동행을 가능하게 해주는 개념이다. 그러한 동행의 기초는 무엇보다도 양자 사이의 수평적 협업과 상호진화이며, 그 진전 가운데서 문학이 정치에 투항하는 정치주의나 그 반대인 탈정치주의의 공간은 점차로 소멸되는 것이다. 조심스럽게나마 우리가 '김현의 시대'를 말하고 상상해볼 수 있다면 아마도 그런 의미에서가 아닐까.

강경석

In order to understand Kim Hyun's poetic world, many handbooks and guidebooks might be required. Certainly, it takes much time and effort to understand even just one of his poems. But they offer something that fascinates us, leading us to make a passionate attempt to interpret them. There is a paradoxical attraction in the overflow that remains in his poems, no matter how much and hard one explains it.... Kim Hyun teaches us that our lives cannot be interpreted unilaterally, that they are uninterpretable substances that can never be fully grasped in one's hands.

An Ji-yeong

[This phrase,] meaning that literature and politics are one in mind, even though they each have a separate body, is a concept that enables the co-traveling of the two in the common vision of "a free and peaceful co-existence among heterogeneities," without negating their individuality. The basis of such co-traveling is, above all, a collateral cooperation and mutual evolution, in which the space for politicism, where literature surrenders to politics, and its opposite, depoliticization, gradually disappear. In this sense, perhaps we can cautiously talk about and imagine "the era of Kim Hyun"?

Kang Kyeong-seok

K-포엣
김현 시선

2018년 8월 13일 초판 1쇄 발행

지은이 김현 | 옮긴이 전승희 | 펴낸이 김재범
편집장 김형욱 | 편집 강민영 | 관리 강초민, 홍희표 | 디자인 나루기획
인쇄·제책 AP프린팅 | 종이 한솔PNS
펴낸곳 (주)아시아 | 출판등록 2006년 1월 27일 제406-2006-000004호
주소 경기도 파주시 회동길 445(서울 사무소: 서울특별시 동작구 서달로 161-1 3층)
전화 02.821.5055 | 팩스 02.821.5057 | 홈페이지 www.bookasia.org
ISBN 979-11-5662-317-5 (set) | 979-11-5662-350-2 (04810)
값은 뒤표지에 있습니다.

K-Poet
Poems by Kim Hyun

Written by Kim Hyun | **Translated by** Jeon Seung-hee
Published by ASIA Publishers | 445, Hoedong-gil, Paju-si, Gyeonggi-do, Korea
(Seoul Office: 161-1, Seodal-ro, Dongjak-gu, Seoul, Korea)
Homepage www.bookasia.org | **Tel** (822).821.5055 | **Fax** (822).821.5057
ISBN 979-11-5662-317-5 (set) | 979-11-5662-350-2 (04810)
First published in Korea by ASIA Publishers 2018

This book is published with the support of the Literature Translation Institute of Korea
(LTI Korea).

K-픽션 한국 젊은 소설

최근에 발표된 단편소설 중 가장 우수하고 흥미로운 작품을 엄선하여 출간하는 〈K-픽션〉은 한국문학의 생생한 현장을 국내외 독자들과 실시간으로 공유하고자 기획되었습니다. 원작의 재미와 품격을 최대한 살린 〈K-픽션〉 시리즈는 매 계절마다 새로운 작품을 선보입니다.

금기와 욕망 Taboo and Desire

71 북소리 - 송영 Drumbeat-Song Yong

72 발칸의 장미를 내게 주었네 - 정미경 He Gave Me Roses of the Balkans-Jung Mi-kyung

73 아무도 돌아오지 않는 밤 - 김숨 The Night Nobody Returns Home-Kim Soom

74 젓가락여자 - 천운영 Chopstick Woman-Cheon Un-yeong

75 아직 일어나지 않은 일 - 김미월 What Has Yet to Happen-Kim Mi-wol

바이링궐 에디션 한국 대표 소설 set 6

운명 Fate

76 언니를 놓치다 - 이경자 Losing a Sister-Lee Kyung-ja

77 아들 - 윤정모 Father and Son-Yoon Jung-mo

78 명두 - 구효서 Relics-Ku Hyo-seo

79 모독 - 조세희 Insult-Cho Se-hui

80 화요일의 강 - 손홍규 Tuesday River-Son Hong-gyu

미의 사제들 Aesthetic Priests

81 고수 - 이외수 Grand Master-Lee Oisoo

82 말을 찾아서 - 이순원 Looking for a Horse-Lee Soon-won

83 상춘곡 - 윤대녕 Song of Everlasting Spring-Youn Dae-nyeong

84 삭매와 자미 - 김별아 Sakmae and Jami-Kim Byeol-ah

85 저만치 혼자서 - 김훈 Alone Over There-Kim Hoon

식민지의 벌거벗은 자들 The Naked in the Colony

86 감자 - 김동인 Potatoes-Kim Tong-in

87 운수 좋은 날 - 현진건 A Lucky Day-Hyŏn Chin'gŏn

88 탈출기 - 최서해 Escape-Ch'oe So-hae

89 과도기 - 한설야 Transition-Han Seol-ya

90 지하촌 - 강경애 The Underground Village-Kang Kyŏng-ae

바이링궐 에디션 한국 대표 소설 set 7

백치가 된 식민지 지식인 Colonial Intellectuals Turned "Idiots"

91 날개 - 이상 Wings-Yi Sang

92 김 강사와 T 교수 - 유진오 Lecturer Kim and Professor T-Chin-O Yu

93 소설가 구보씨의 일일 - 박태원 A Day in the Life of Kubo the Novelist-Pak Taewon

94 비 오는 길 - 최명익 Walking in the Rain-Ch'oe Myŏngik

95 빛 속에 - 김사량 Into the Light-Kim Sa-ryang